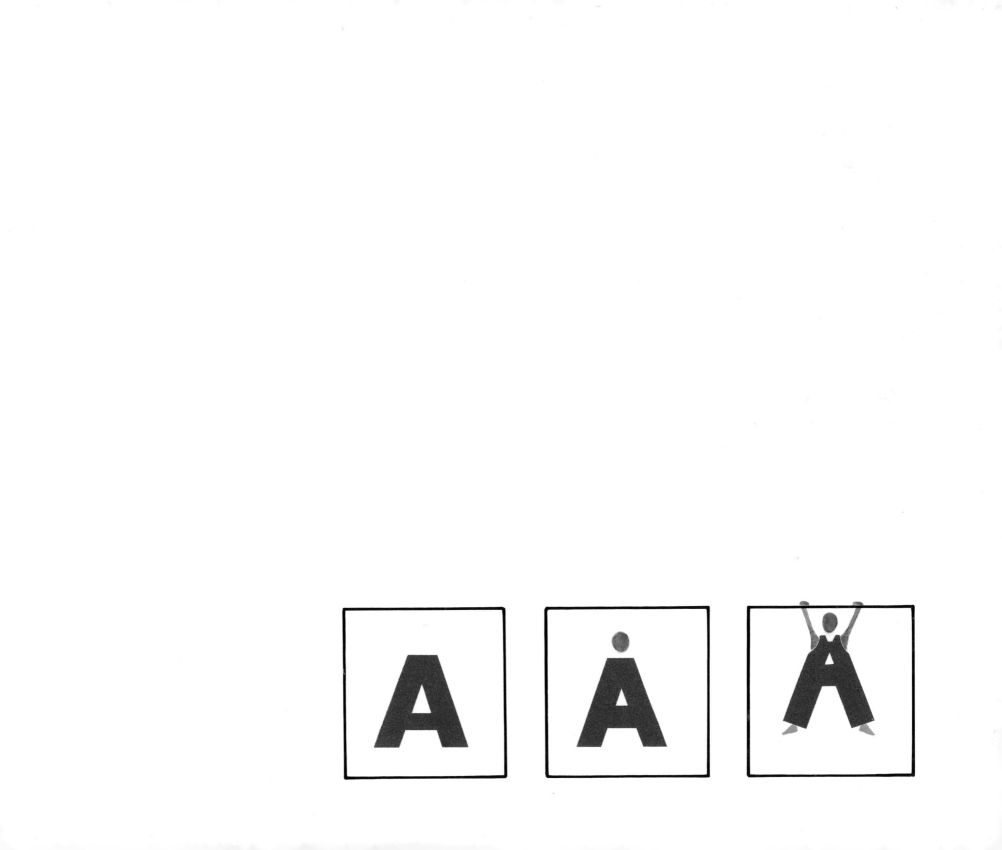

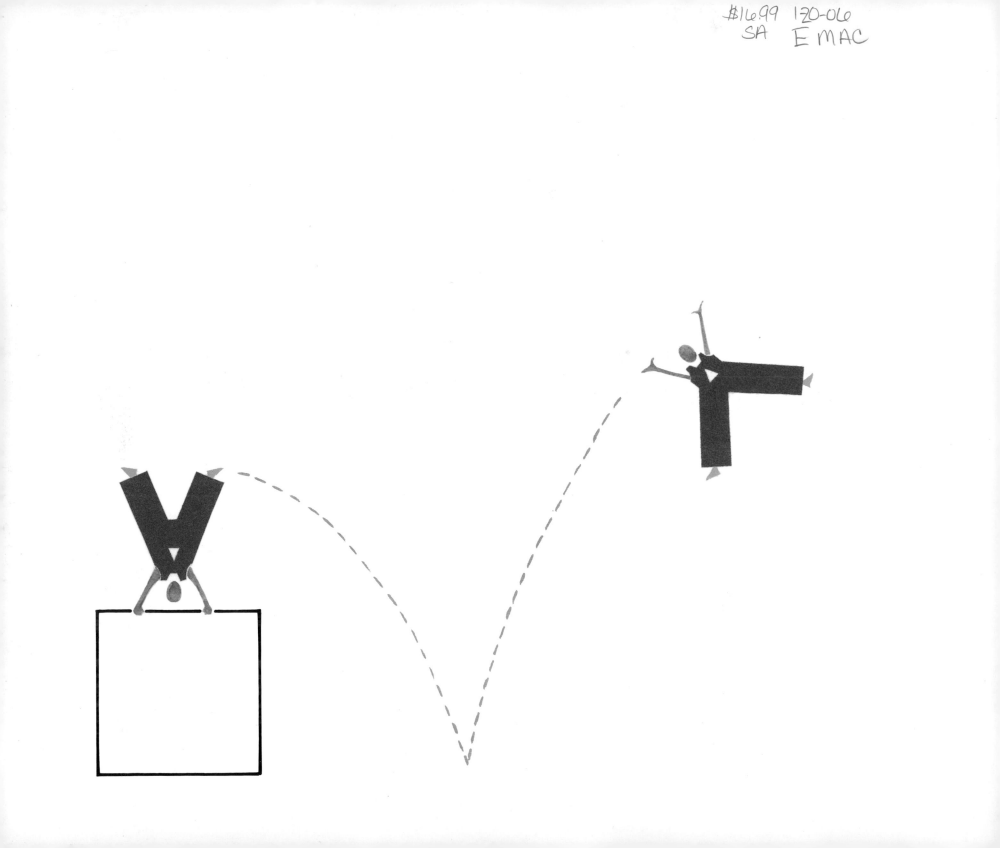

ALPHABATICS

Suse MacDonald

Aladdin Paperbacks

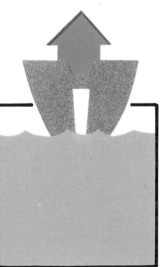

Ark

Bb

balloon

Cc

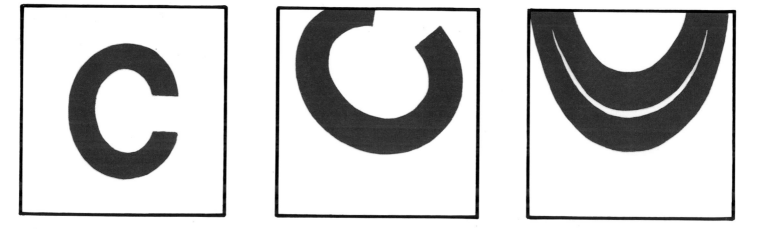

Clown

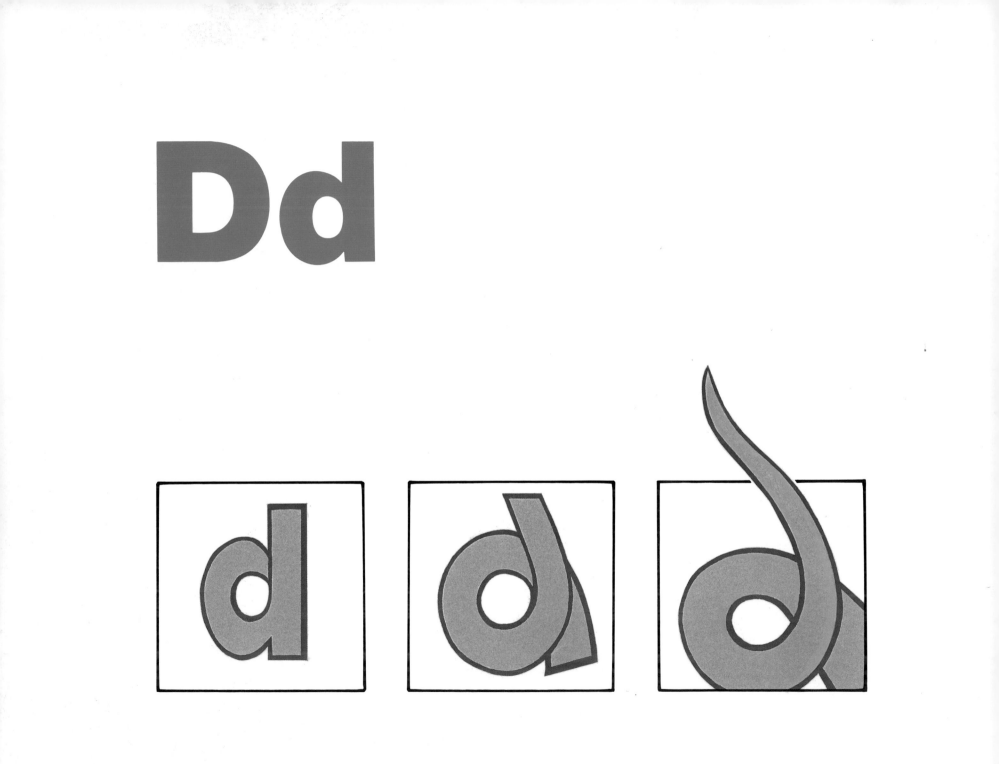

dragon

Elephant

Fish

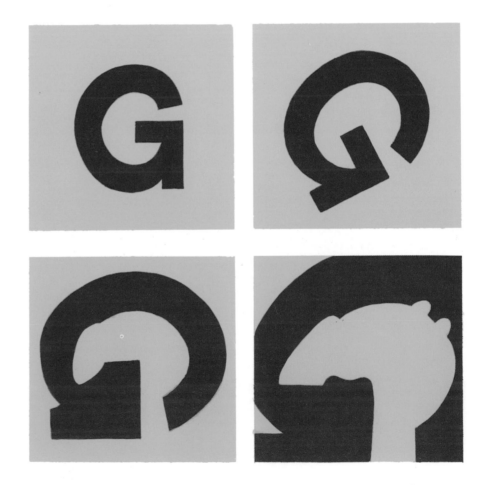

Giraffe

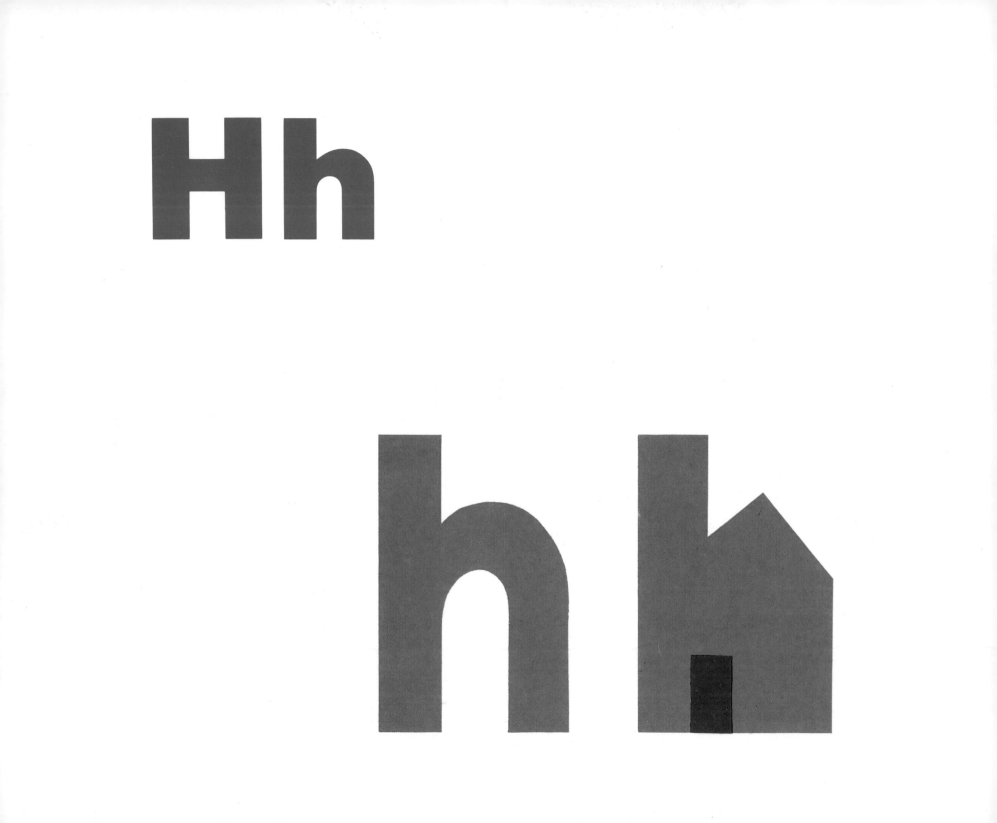

house

insect

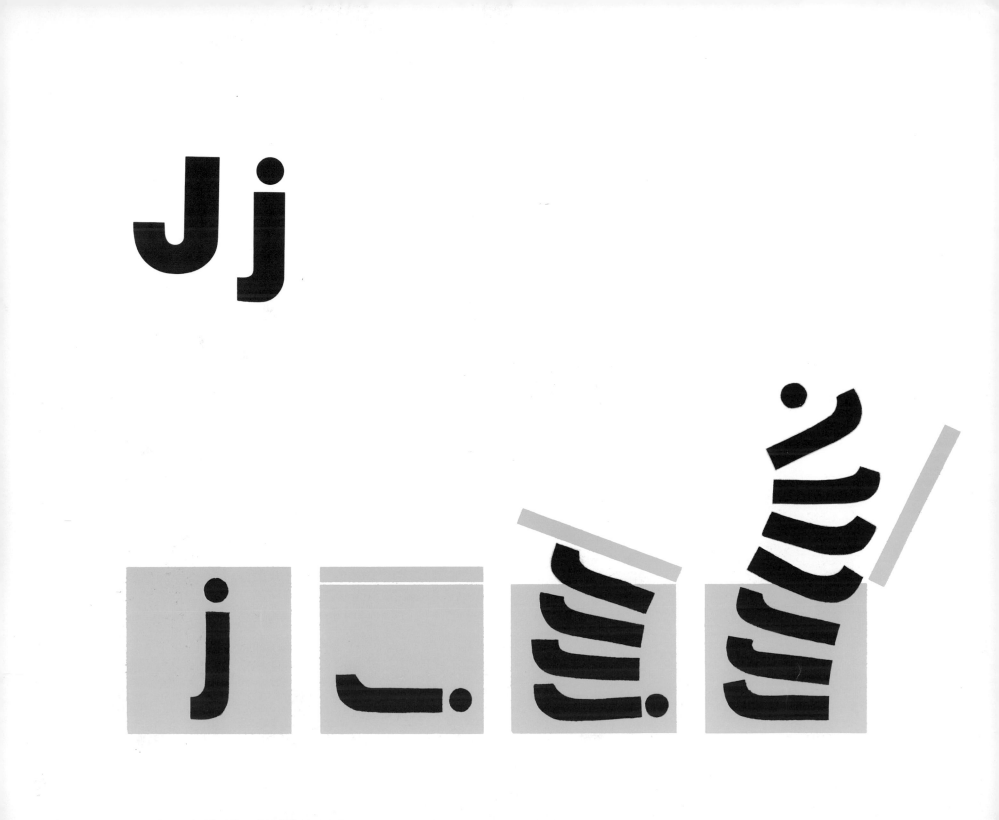

jack-
in-the-box

Kite

Ll

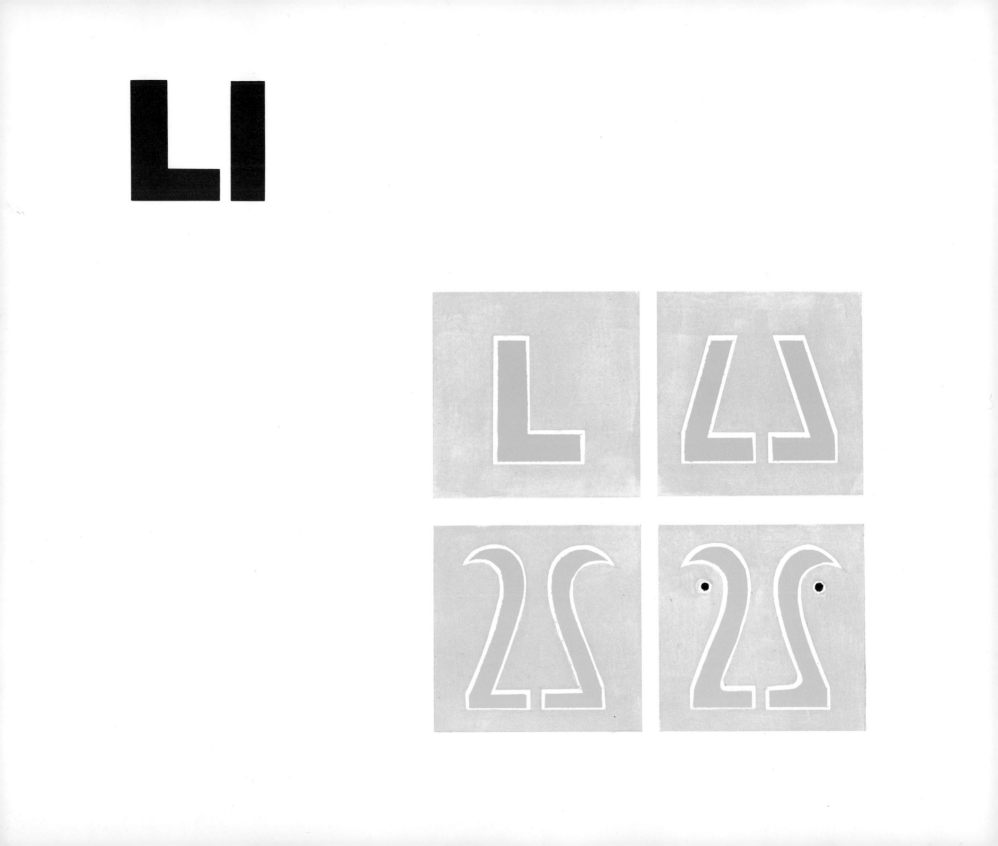

Lion

mustache

nest

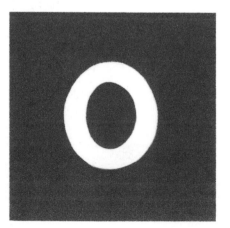  

owl

Plane

Qq

Quail

Rr

rooster

Swan

Tree

umbrella

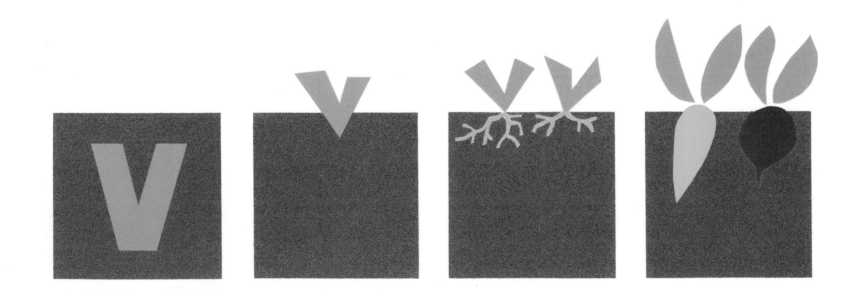

Vegetables

Ww

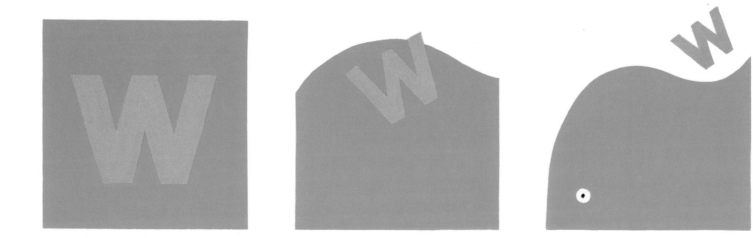

Whale

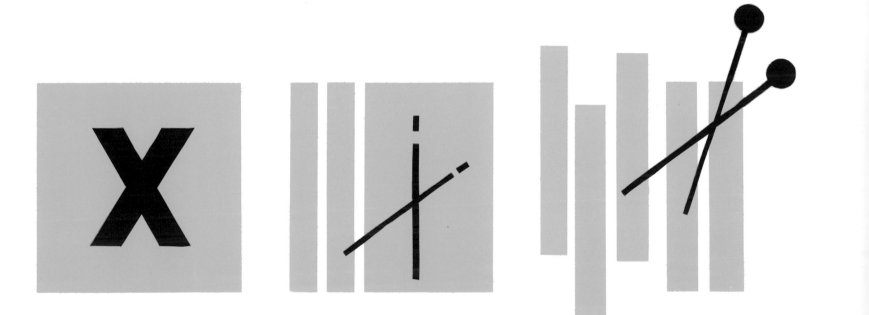
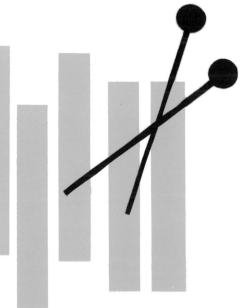

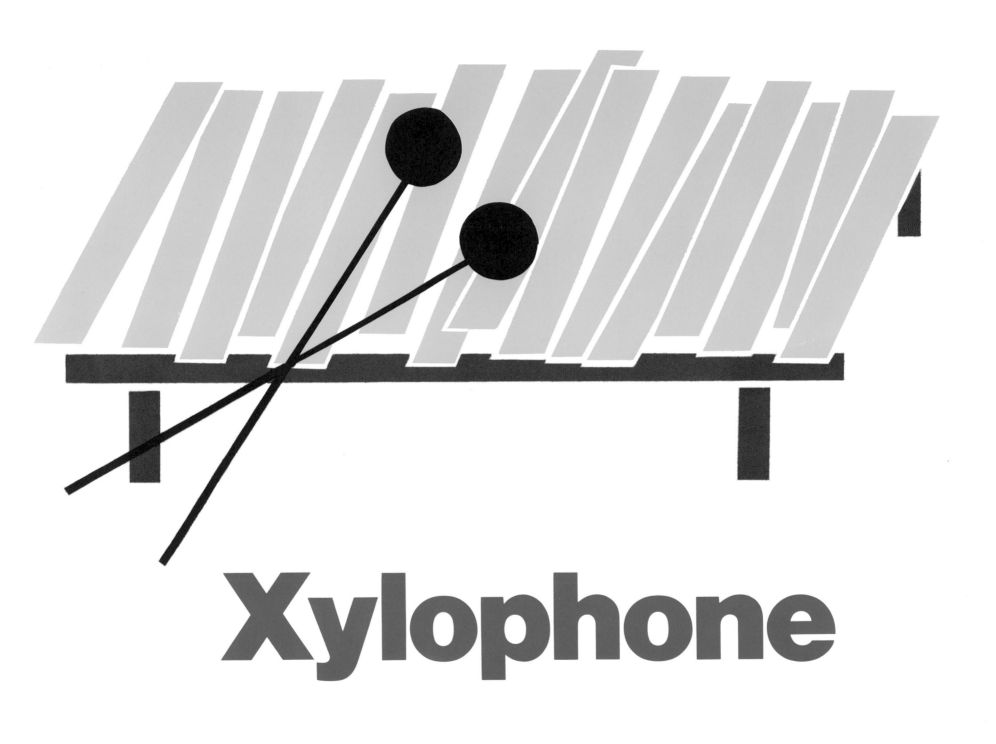

Xylophone

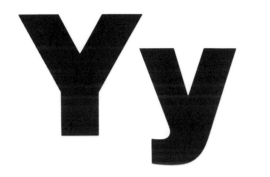

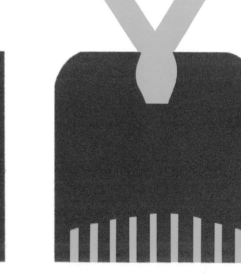

Yak

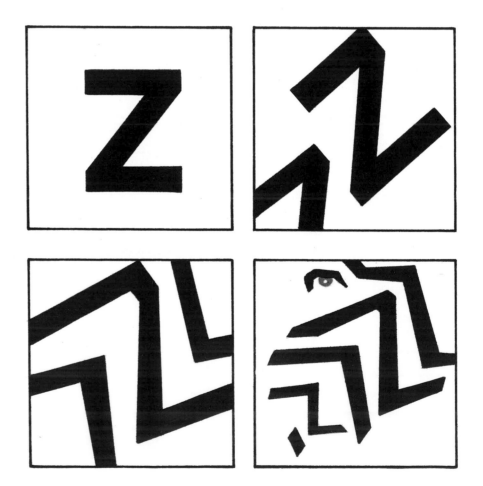

Zebra

For Stuart, with special thanks to Susan and Deborah

Aladdin Paperbacks. An imprint of Simon & Schuster Children's Publishing Division, 1230 Avenue of the Americas, New York, NY 10020. Copyright © 1986 by Suse MacDonald. All rights reserved including the right of reproduction in whole or in part in any form. First Aladdin Paperbacks edition, 1992. Also available in a hardcover edition from Simon & Schuster Books for Young Readers. Printed in Hong Kong. 10   9

Library of Congress Cataloging-in-Publication Data MacDonald, Suse. Alphabatics / by Suse MacDonald. — 1st Aladdin Books ed. p. cm. Originally published: New York : Bradbury Press, 1986. Summary: The letters of the alphabet are transformed and incorporated into twenty-six illustrations, so that the hole in "b" becomes a balloon and "y" turns into the head of a yak. ISBN 0-689-71625-7   1. English Language—Alphabet—Juvenile literature.   [1. Alphabet.] I. Title.   PE1155.M3   1992   [E]—dc20   91-38497